Caroline L. Wallace

Santiago de Cuba before the War

Caroline L. Wallace

Santiago de Cuba before the War

ISBN/EAN: 9783337378783

Printed in Europe, USA, Canada, Australia, Japan

Cover: Foto ©Andreas Hilbeck / pixelio.de

More available books at **www.hansebooks.com**

SANTIAGO DE CUBA

BEFORE THE WAR;

OR,

RECUERDOS DE SANTIAGO.

BY

CAROLINE L. WALLACE.

Neely's Booklet Library, No. 4. *Jan. 23, 1899. Issued Weekly, $5 per year. Entered as second-class matter at N. Y. Post Office.*

F. TENNYSON NEELY,

PUBLISHER,

LONDON.   NEW YORK.

PREFACE.

HAVING passed several happy years in this "Siempre Fiel Isla" before the unfortunate animosity between the people inhabiting it had developed into savageness; ere the pomp and pride of Spain had been humbled, and its fruitful lands devastated by the vengeance of its native born inhabitants; when all was fair and quaint and fascinating, with a glamour all its own, I found that this "Pearl of the Antilles," cradled upon the calm waters of the Caribbean, clothed in the gorgeous verdure of the tropics, and fanned by soft southern breezes, extended a hospitable hand of greeting to the stranger attracted hither, in search of new and foreign scenes.

With charming memories of the gracious hospitality of the Cubans, as well as of the stately courtesy of the Spaniards with whom I was thrown, I am tempted to embody a few recollections of those happy days, that have impressed themselves upon my memory in never fading pictures, whose glowing lights and brilliant colors shine out undimmed among the many scenes that time has hung around this gallery of gems.

Now that Cuba can no longer be considered the "fairest gem in the crown of Spain," and the Stars and Stripes float where the red and gold of Spain long proudly waved, I can but waft one sigh of regret to those departed days on that once tranquil island, which will so soon take on the work and hurry and onward march of improvement that kills out all picturesqueness, all romance, with its metallic nineteenth century advancement.

C. L. W.

August, 1898.

CONTENTS.

SANTIAGO DE CUBA
BEFORE THE WAR.

I.

ARRIVAL AT SANTIAGO DE CUBA.

On Sunday, the 6th of October, 18—, in the early morning, we came in sight of Morro Castle, which crowns the heights on the right, at the narrow entrance of the tortuous way, that, with many windings and turnings, leads up to the bay of Santiago de Cuba.

Its yellow walls, embrowned turrets and time-stained battlements surmount the abrupt height which rises from the sea, its threatening air dominating with ancient imperiousness the narrow entrance.

The rocky base, deep moat, and huge draw-bridge, of the fifteenth century, form a frowning, though most pictuesque object against the blue background of a cloudless sky; with the green waters of the sea curling around its base, and the red and yellow colors of the Spanish flag waving from its apex, while its black-mouthed guns, rusty with the moisture of ages, point savagely at the bold intruder, who would dare to brave their anger.

Excavated out of solid rock upon which this ancient fortress stands, were the cells, offices, and torture chambers of the inquisition, used in the times when the "Holy Office" assumed to be arbiter of all Spanish America.

Diagonally across the outer entrance of the harbor, to the west of "Morro," and opposite to the fortress of Santa Catalina, stands the Castle of La Zocapa, on Cañones Point.

As we pass close beneath the walls, it seems as though there was hardly room for another vessel to enter, a distance of not more than one hundred and twenty yards lying between the opposing shores.

Any hostile vessel essaying to enter the harbor of Santiago would not only be subjected to the fire of "Morro," and the water battery below and behind, to the east of this castle, but would also run the gauntlet of La Estrella, Santa Catalina and Zocapa, and in addition,

Thus, Santiago is eminently fitted by nature to be a western Gibraltar; and, next to that of Rio de Janeiro, the bay of Santiago de Cuba is decidedly the most picturesque on the western hemisphere.

The hills that rise on either side are crowned with palms and cocoa trees, the yellow blossom of the century plant making a perpetual golden glow. Cacti, prickly pear, mangoes, bamboo, the cotton plant, with flowering vines innumerable, riot luxuriously in all the security of perpetual summer that knows no change, fears no decay, nor winter blasts.

The faint trace of the early morning mist, still hanging around these verdure clad shores, was fast melting away beneath the ardent kiss of the fiery god whose warm embrace misses no spot nor blossom in his morning salutation.

As we approach the city, the wide waters of the bay spread out before us, calm as a mirror. The wharves and custom-house buildings—from the moment she had well passed Morillo Point, be subjected to an enfilading fire from Punta Gorda, and, as soon as the narrowest point was reached, to another from Isla de Smith.

large, low structures, with wide sheds, and red tiled roofs—the blue and white coated Cara-bineros, with their wide somberos and red rosettes—badge of their authority, are the first objects of our attention.

After much deliberation, for hurry is a thing unknown in Spanish countries, we disembark. Several stalwart negroes, clothed in the fashion of Paradise, with the addition only of scant garments about the loins, their dark skins shining, and smooth as ebony, their great muscles standing out, strong and vigorous as Hercules, seize upon our trunks, bags and im-pedimenta, and, regardless of size or weight, hoist them up on to their heads, and start off up the steep and stony street that leads to our hotel.

There are no hacks, cabs or carriages of any description awaiting the traveler as he steps upon terra firma; and your choice of getting your luggage carried lies between the negro who takes it on his head and a small caretta, or two-wheeled cart, harnessed to a mule that looks as though he might succumb even to its diminutive proportions, that squeak and rattle as it is jolted over the rough stones, in spite of the numerous ropes with which it is bound together.

Walking up the narrow street, creeping along on the shady side, as we regard the one-story houses and strange aspect of things in general we feel as though we had been landed back a century or two in the past.

Apartments had been engaged for us at the Hotel del Commercio, and we were glad to find ourselves within the shelter of its thick walls and substantial floors after so many days of discomfort on board the small Spanish steamer that had brought us from Havana.

Our first breakfast in Santiago was a gastronomic delight, the variety and service of the dishes leaving nothing to be desired; "Monsieur Jean," the head waiter, with true French tact helping us so daintily and deftly that it was a pleasure to have him moving about.

At the head of the table we found Colonel C——, whose nine years' residence there had so imbued him with the spirit of the place that he seemed a part of it; his genial atmosphere giving an added charm to these quaint and unique surroundings. Here, also, we met the

handsome Spanish officer whose grave and
dignified demeanor had so impressed us on
board the steamer. Over whom and what he
might be I had myself inwardly much specu-
lated. With true Spanish courtesy he recog-
nized us as his companions de voyage, making
a graceful salutation as we took our places at
the table.

Although the foreign element was in prepon-
derance, there were several English-speaking
gentlemen among them, who, with the ease of
manner and social instincts of the Latin races,
did not fail to make everything as agreeable as
possible to the newcomers.

Our breakfast consisted of almost as many
courses as a dinner, and every one smoked
cigarettes between them, finishing with black
coffee and cigars, sitting over them, and pro-
longing the conversation until nearly noon.

Breakfast over, we went out into the corridor in front, which seemed to take the place
of a parlor or reception room, as a point of re-
union. Here, whoever came to call waited for
his friend to come out, in case he should still
be at table. To my surprise, several small
Cuban horses, all saddled and bridled, were

tied to the railing, patiently awaiting their owners, who had been breakfasting within.

A commingling of tongues strikes the ear like the music of varied instruments, as this gathering from many lands join in animated conversation; and though but an hour or two ago we were all strangers, one to another, a sympathetic chord, the result of kindly feeling and courteous speech, vibrates through the whole company.

A spacious, lofty apartment on the ground floor, had been assigned to us, with windows looking out upon the theater opposite; the first story of which was a deep brownish red, and the second a bright blue, with much white decoration on façade, doors and cornices. The broad flight of wide stone stairs and terrace leading up to it appeared to be the rendezvous for many colored nurses with their charges, from the baby at the breast to the three and five year old tots, who enjoyed unrestrained possession of their playground, their little chemises twisted up into a narrow wisp about their waists with a knot behind, which the nurse's outstretched hand held tightly, and kept them from falling or straying away into danger.

Our other windows, and also doors, opened upon the patio, around which we had to pass in going to the dining room, which was upon another street at a different altitude, so that we were obliged to ascend a flight of stairs to reach the corridor that led to it.

The visitors from the haciendas who could not reach town by railway (there being only one in any direction) were obliged to come in on horseback; around this lower patio their animals were tied, and patiently awaited their owners; an occasional donkey adding his sonorous voice to the neighing and stamping of the horses.

The loud voices of the drivers and attendants in Creole-French and Spanish, the numerous passers-in-and-out of all sorts, formed a curious conglomeration of sounds and sights that kept one on the *qui vive* of expectation, wondering what would come next in the strange panorama that was constantly changing before our astonished gaze.

II.

MANNERS AND HABITS.

THE long day in Santiago begins early, for with the first sunrise all business and working people are astir; and although in this indolent atmosphere nobody hurries, everything begins at an hour that to an American seems unearthly.

By three or four o'clock in the morning one is awakened by the patter of the small hoofs of mules that come in long strings of perhaps thirty or forty, each tied to the tail of the one in front of him, and laden almost out of sight with fruits, vegetables and produce from the neighboring haciendas or estates, which are sent into supply the market, from which all the city buys its daily rations of food and provisions for man and beast.

The colored servants of every shade, from darkest mahogany up to palest yellow, with blue eyes and crinkly, light hair, erect, and with stately grace, are moving about in the early morning; the crowning bit of bright color in the inevitable bandanna (which becomes a part of their costume even in tender years) making a gorgeous setting for their dark skins. Their long trailing skirts of bright-hued cotton, well starched, rustle over the pavements to the accompanying sluff-sluff of shoes down at the heel, that clatter along, as laden with trays and baskets they go to bring from the market the day's provisions.

After a cup of coffee and a roll the merchant, banker, or commissioner, in lightest of clothing, neatly and elegantly dressed, sets out for his place of business downtown, the ladies and children taking their coffee or chocolate in flowing and loosest of dishabille, in most unceremonious fashion, for the real breakfast is not before ten or perhaps later, when the gentlemen of the house, having had three or four hours devoted to business, are ready to return and breakfast at leisure with the family.

A Creole breakfast consists usually of five or six courses, beginning with rice and eggs, fried plantains, delicious fish, beefsteak, buniata (a vegetable similar to sweet potatoes)

salad, fruits, and some sweet dish, with red
wine, ending with excellent coffee; the smoking of cigarettes always accompanying every
meal.

In the middle of the day comes the siesta,
indispensable to the early riser who has been
up and at work, before the heat came on, as
also to the languorous señora who has rocked
all day in her easy chair and been fanned by
her servant, or perchance done a little fancy
work, or studied her music lesson, and played
with the half naked baby that its black nurse
brings her to admire.

Heavy curtains hang before the wide, iron
barred windows which project outward into
the street, and admitting of conversation with
the passer-by, are the scene of many inter-
views, filled with telling glances and fervid ex-
pressions that, later on, develop into attach-
ments which, with the ardent Creole temperament, expand like flowers beneath the sun
into the full bloom of maturity with tropical
rapidity.

As the Creole señorita is not supposed to receive or converse with young men, except in
the presence of some older member of the

family, etiquette not even permitting her to sit beside, but always opposite, her visitor, she does not fail to avail herself of the opportunity of the friendly window, with its half-drawn curtain and wide-apart bars, which allow of so near an approach to the one who has been walking up and down, waiting for the happy moment when his inamorata shall appear in response to his desires.

A gracious hospitality characterizes Creole manners. Even though the first salutation: "A los pies de Usted," to which you reply: "Beso Usted la mano," seems a somewhat exaggerated expression, much cordiality and evident amiability make you feel at home within their borders, and a simplicity of manner and freedom of conversation contribute to a feeling of well-being most grateful to one in a strange land.

At the entrance of a house one is apt to encounter lolling about the door negroes of all ages and sizes, and in the hall you pass the elegant volante, with its immense wheels and long shafts, glittering lanterns and rich upholstery, which is always driven directly into the house after it has given the señoritas an outing, and there stands a gorgeous witness to its owner's financial status.

One peculiarity of Cuban houses is the single entrance, for, being built with a patio or court, on to which all the rooms open, the great door upon the street, which swings open wide enough to admit the volante and pair of mules, affords entrance and exit for all that pertains to housekeeping as well as for all visitors from the highest to the lowest degree.

I frequently saw the elegant Doctor de L——, on his return from his morning round of visits, dismount on the sidewalk, and, throwing the bridle upon his horse's neck, pass up the steps into his house, followed by his gentle horse, who walked up after his master as tamely as a dog.

A Cuban *ménage* is simplicity itself compared with American life, and in passing one may look in through the great windows and open doors, screened during the middle of the day by heavy curtains of striped linen that keep out the sun but flap in the wind and show glimpses of the whole picture of domestic life as you pass along the street.

Evening descends early after the red sun

has hidden behind the hills across the bay, leaving his crimson glow upon the placid waters; no long twilight lingers here, but night, with dusky wings, swoops down, making a quick transition from the tropic day.

With darkness comes the refreshing land breeze; and the social nature of the Creole incites to visit with his neighbors and the "tertulias," or gathering together of near friends, fill the streets with cheerful voices and merry laughter. Often whole families and their visitors are seated out on the sidewalk in front of their houses, from the grandmother down to the five-year-old, all chatting and smoking, the señoras as well as the men, including the little boys.

The shops are open, and much of the buying is done at evening; the merchant, in most familiar fashion, addressing you by your first name and inquiring after your family as in a social visit; and, if purchases are made, some little thing is offered as a "ñape" or present, thrown in to bind the bargain. If it is not offered, the shopper does not hesitate to ask for his little gift, which it would look small to refuse. The merchant accompanies you to the door, and bows you out, with the compliments of leave taking and good wishes.

The name of the owner does not appear upon the sign above the door, but the name of the store, as "La Puerta del Sol," "La Caridad," "Le Monte de Oro," "El Paradiso," etc.

The Plaza de Armas, in front of the palace, on certain evenings is filled with promenaders, who go to listen to the music of the military bands. Here one meets all one's acquaintances, and enjoys what is called the "opera economique," for the Cubans are a music-loving people, and the Spanish regimental bands give a programme that is a delight to listen to.

The ladies, with true Creole *dolce far niente*, remain seated until the last number, which is usually a Cuban danza; even not hesitating in passing before a gentleman occupying a seat they may desire, to stop before him, and, with a movement of the head, indicate that she would like his seat. He is in duty bound to rise and offer it, and she accepts as a matter of course. But when the "danza" strikes up all the ladies arise, and in twos and threes, begin to promenade around the plaza; the gentlemen taking their vacated seats, and enjoying in their turn the pleasure of looking at and, perchance, criticizing the ladies. Those not fortunate enough to secure seats form in a line opposite their more favored brothers, and between this phalanx of admiring eyes all the promenaders have to pass. Although a Cuban lady seldom walks, there is a remarkable undulating grace of movement, rythmic and swaying, harmonizing with the languorous air and peculiar passion of the Cuban ''danza.''

With the ''Danza,'' the Retrata closes. The band marches through the streets to the barracks, playing to the end. The plashing fountains and fragrant jasmines remain sole possessors of the now empty Plaza.

Ten o'clock is the usual hour for the closing of houses, and all visitors expect to leave at that time. Indeed, all down the street one hears the banging of the heavy doors as regularly as the striking of the clock.

Then sally forth the ''sereños,'' or watchmen, picturesque in the white uniforms, with long pikes and lanterns, calling out, in musical tones, the hours and quarters, and at the same time the state of the weather as ''Las dies, y ser-e-no!'' ''Las nueve, y nu-bla-do!'' ''Las doce, y estrell-a-da esta la no-che!'' so that, at whatever hour during the night one chances to be awake, one can know with certainty the time and the conditions that prevail. They have a way of singing out the hours that leaves a long echo behind as they pass down the street that lingers lovingly on the soft night air, till it dies out upon your ear as you fall back into the land of dreams with a feeling of security that without, as well as within, ''Esta la noche serena.''

III.

SUNDAY IN SANTIAGO.

SUNDAY is a *fête* day in Santiago. Very early in the morning the bells ring out with a joyous clamor, calling the devout to prayers. The ringing is not done by pulling a bell rope, but by striking with a metal rod upon the bell itself—a repetition of rapid uneven strokes, producing a singular effect, which seems to say, "Hurry up, hurry up, and come to church."

After attending mass it is not unusual for visits to be paid and received. In fact, even the religious functions at the cathedral and at the Misa de Tropa, which is celebrated at the San Francisco, have more the air of social gatherings than of religious services.

The center of the church is filled with ladies in fine attire; a black lace mantilla, which falls partially over the face like a veil, taking the place of a bonnet, which is not considered appropriate in church here.

Servants carrying low chairs and rugs accompany their mistresses, and after spreading the rugs and placing the chairs upon them, they with careful hands draw out the folds of flowing skirts, so that no effect shall be lost upon the critical observer who may be seated behind or at the side.

Here the matronly señora, in all the beauty of full-blown maturity, with dark flashing eyes, now half concealed behind the lowered veil, with jeweled fingers parts the sacred beads as she repeats her "Padre Nuestro," while her young daughter, just blossoming into girlhood at her side, looks out with shy but ardent glances at the young lieutenant, fresh from Spain, trim and erect in his gold bands and bright buttons, that have not yet been tarnished in his country's service, who, leaning against a column not far away, is not insensible to the language of her eyes, and answers back flash for flash. All around the sides of the church stand the military, while a few pews or seats in front only are reserved for the high functionaries and foreign consuls. The dark and

wrinkled duenna, whose flashing eyes alone recall her departed youth, does not fail to fulfill
her accustomed part in the general devotions.
Numerous colored servants in Sunday garb,
and bright bandana turbaned heads, stand
piously behind their mistresses. All around
the entrance and massed between the arches
stand the troops, resplendent in gay uniforms.

As this is the Misa de Tropa, the regimental
bands take a prominent part in the music, and
in addition to organ and choir give a gorgeous
coloring to this part of the ceremonies.

When the services are over, the military are
the first to leave the church. They stand
around outside, in front of the entrance, awaiting the exit of the señoras, looking for recognition and probably exchange of salutations, if
not in expectation of some word perhaps, in
soto voce, intimating an intention to be at the
retrata in the evening, or on the Alameda at
the usual afternoon promenade, where the marine band plays about 5 o'clock.

On the way home from church it is quite
usual to pay friendly visits, even as early as
9 or 10 o'clock in the morning.

Late in the afternoon, toward sunset, all the

world flocks to the cool Alameda, where under the shade of overspreading trees which border the broad alleys, in sight of the beautiful waters of the bay and the distant hills that rise upon the opposite shore, those fortunate enough to be possessed of volantes drive up and down, and listen to the strains of the marine band that gives its Sunday concert there. Those who do not ride sit around upon the stone seats, fanned by the soft sea breeze, or saunter up and down in the shade of the trees till the promenade is over.

The volante is the only carriage known in Santiago de Cuba, and a most luxurious and comfortable affair it is. The body is fashioned like a chaise, with top that is deep enough to cover the whole till its occupants are completely hidden from sight, or can be thrown entirely back, leaving in full view the señora, who, without wrap or bonnet, reclines luxuriously upon its upholstered cushions, her elegant toilette in full evidence from the tips of her small boots to the crown of her head. The single seat is wide enough for three ladies to ride comfortably.

The body of the carriage hangs upon strong

leather straps that extend inside the long shafts, giving a delightful swaying motion that avoids all jolting as it is drawn over the pavement. The two immense wheels are placed so far behind the swinging body that the costumes of the occupants can be outspread to their fullest extent without risk of being soiled from contact with dust or mud.

Gayly caparisoned mules, with much silver plating upon their harnesses, and with tails and manes braided and tied up with ribbons, draw these vehicles. One mule is harnessed between the thills, while the other is entirely outside, and carries the calesero or driver, who rides upon his back while he directs them both.

The calesero is as conspicious in his appearance as the rest of the equipage, with his much-braided jacket, white breeches, and high top patent-leather boots. With whip in hand and gathered reins he urges on his little beasts with many quips and quirks, in language incomprehensible to any other than mulish ears.

On Sunday evening there is always music in the Plaza. There congregate whole families in gala attire. They sit around in groups, chat-

ting and listening to the music of the regimental band, which begins to play at 8
o'clock and closes promptly at 10.

The blue façade and Moorish architecture of
the governor's palace stand out distinctly, outlined by rows of gasjets, showing its broad
portals and arching windows, its white cornices, pilasters and balconies in bold relief
against the dark background of the evening
sky.

There is no chill or dampness in the air, and
no wraps are needed. The young señoritas,
in lightest of muslins and organdies, in trailing
skirts, with gleaming shoulders and arms, walk
joyously about, enjoying the freshness of the
evening, with no other covering on their heads
than their own dark hair.

Here sociability and flirtation reign. The
Cuban *jeuness dorè*, as well as the large con-
tingent of Spanish officials, in immaculate
evening attire, promenade up and down, looking the things they dare not say, as they pass
the objects of their admiration, seated in close
proximity to parental or family guardianship;
while the soft fluttering fans, in the expressive
language so well understood by Spanish women

everywhere, indicate the sentiments of those using them as plainly as do spoken words.

The young men generally walk about during the evening, until the final danza is played when the ladies promenade up and down with all the insouciance and nonchalance of women who would be surprised if in the passing "viva la elegancia!" "via la gracia!" "que hermosura!" and a thousand other flattering compliments were not expressed.

The danza finished, the band strikes up the stately Marcha Real, and with measured tread marches off down the narrow streets, playing as it goes, the sounds growing fainter and fainter until it reaches the barracks and the last note dies out.

In a few moments every one has departed, and the Plaza is deserted, but the plashing fountains still play on, and the sensuous fragrance of the tropic night still lingers beneath the starry vault.

IV.

EL COBRE AND THE MIRACULOUS VIRGIN.

Leaving Santiago by the small steamer Fedrico, we cross over to "Punta Sal," where we take the railroad for El Cobre, some twelve miles distant. Here are located the Cobre copper mines, perhaps the richest in the world, and certainly the first ever worked by Europeans on this continent, they having been opened in 1524. Here we saw the begrimed and blackened miners ascending and descending in their cages, drawn by means of ropes from the depths below, and far underneath the surface of the heated earth; the shafts extending over a thousand feet under ground.

El Cobre is celebrated quite as much for its "Miraculous Virgin of Charity," as for its copper mines—thousands of people making pilgrimages there from all parts of the world, in hope of being cured of ills and diseases of all sorts.

This "Miraculous Virgin" was discovered floating upon the water in the vicinity of this coast, so the story goes, was picked up, and carried into a church and placed upon the altar, but evidently this was not the spot intended for the abode of this supernatural occupant, for suddenly it disappeared from the church, and was afterward found calmly reposing upon the site of the one which was later built for it, and where it has ever since remained.

The church stands upon an eminence, and in order to reach it one has to ascend several terraces paved with brick—up several wide flights of stairs which extend the whole length of these terraces.

Up and down these terraces pilgrims are coming and going at all hours of the day; many of them making the whole ascent upon their knees, the better to demonstrate the piety of their pilgrimage.

As many come from great distances, some overland and on horseback, at cost of much fatigue, large comfortable hostelries have been erected near the church for their accommodation.

Architecturally the church is not remarkable, being a rather plain edifice built of brick. The chief attraction centers in the "Miraculous Virgin," although to me the massive chains of marvelous workmanship in beautifully-wrought silver (which had been sent from Spain) hanging from the ceiling, and to which were attached the lamps by which it is illuminated, were the object of greatest admiration.

Suspended from some of these beautiful silver chains were large pans, filled with oil in which wax tapers were floating around and constantly burning. I saw many persons come up, and with a large spoon, after carefully pushing away the small bits of floating straw, tiny insects and gnats that had accumulated, take out a spoonful of the consecrated oil, and saying a prayer or two, swallow it. Others would fill a small vial with it and carry it away, in full faith that its healing properties would work the wonders they so much desired upon some sick child or invalid left at home.

Before partaking of the blessed oil, however, all had knelt before the sacred image and in prayer invoked her blessing.

This diminutive image in wood, for it is not more than twelve or fifteen inches in height, stands on the right of the altar. Inclosed in glass, with locked door, it is visible from all sides. All around at its feet are jewels innumerable and of immense worth that have been brought and laid there as offerings in gratitude for miraculous favors bestowed.

We were conducted to a large room behind the sacristy which was devoted to the purpose of preserving the hundreds of testimonials, such as crutches that had been thrown aside by their owners, who had not for years walked without them, but had been instantly cured and gone off, having no further use for them, leaving them behind as evidence of their marvelous restoration.

One young man was cited, who, after years of helpless invalidism, had made a vow that if he was restored to health he would devote the rest of his life to good works, was brought in upon a mattress and laid before the virgin, and was healed; he arose and walked out of the church, joined the troops then fighting in Santo Domingo, and was still doing valiant duty in the army.

Magnificent gifts of all descriptions were shown us that had been brought in grateful recognition of benefits received.

Drawer after drawer was opened by the courteous padre, who displayed to us the costly garments of rich fabrics, covered with heavy embroidery in gold that stood out in high relief, solid as sculptured marble.

Incredible seemed the treasures of money and jewels and precious things that had been lavished upon this small wooden image. But more wonderful still seemed the *unknown power behind* this frail object that had so influenced with believing faith the many souls that had with reverent hopes sought and found the fulfillment of their prayers.

Here also there were for sale small gold medalions with an effigy of the virgin on one side, with the inscription "Mater Caritatis," and on the reverse the church crowning these terraces and many stairs, and this inscription: "Puis te hizo la trinidad tan perfecta y sin egual, Librar nos de todo mal Virgin de la Caridad," which translated signifies, "Since thou wert made by the Trinity perfect and without equal, deliver us from all evil, Virgin of Charity."

I was myself so imbued with the spirit of the place that I immediately possessed myself of one of these sacred medals, and attached it to my watch chain, where it has hung ever since as a mascot, as well as a souvenir of my visit to El Cobre.

V.

CUBAN WOMEN.

CUBAN women, or, as they call themselves, Creoles, are usually very good looking. Indeed, among young women it is rare to see a homely one. With dark eyes and hair abundant and curling and pale complexions with regular features, they possess a type of beauty all their own. The children are little fat cherubs of the Murillo type, and run about untrammeled by clothing until they are seven or eight years old. Nothing prettier than a young girl just blooming into adolescence can be imagined; a little older they incline to embonpoint, and I will remark *en passant* that flesh is an important factor in beauty here. To be slender and thin is considered ugly and worthy of commiseration. Neither is color desirable. An additional whiteness is obtained by a free use of cascarilla, a cosmetic prepared here from fine white shells, ground up into an impalpable powder, which is abundantly and generously applied, and even if visible and thick enough to rub off upon a gentleman's coat sleeve nothing is thought of it, as it is in universal use. Rouge is never used.

Fine shoulders, beautifully molded arms, small hands and feet, with the typical high-arched Spanish instep, complete the ensemble. Easy, graceful manners, and fine voices, musical and trainante, with much vivacity and gesture, expressive features, emphasized by little movements of the hands and shoulder shrugs, render them charmingly piquant. There seems to be no awkward period in the life of a Creole girl, for from the opening bud to the full-blown flower, the interval is short.

At fourteen a girl is considered marriageable, and is never permitted to go out alone, and even after an engagement is declared, she never receives her *fiancé*, except in the presence of some older member of the family. He may accompany her to the theater, concert or bull-fight, but always with the family.

If the parents oppose a marriage, the lover may *steal* her—of course the robbery is committed with her own consent—and deposit her allowed to visit her under the usual conditional in the house of a mutual friend, where he is etiquette, until the time necessary for taking all the preliminary steps preparatory for the marriage has expired. Once taken away from her parents' house parental authority cannot prevail against the marriage.

Large families are not considered objectionable, but, on the contrary, many children are the precious jewels in the crown of motherhood.

When quite a little girl the Cuban maid has a playmate among the colored children, chosen from the servants or slaves of her own age, who grows up with her in the double capacity of companion and servant, and who, when she marries, goes with her as her own attendant to her new abode.

Creole women are frank and affectionate by nature, and do not hesitate by word or glance to show their admiration—the concealment, skirmishing and flirtation practiced by Americans being quite unknown.

When a man falls in love with a girl he at once declares his sentiments to her parents and asks permission to visit her; thus all embarrassment is avoided.

A marriage in church often takes place at

midnight or very early in the morning, avoiding publicity, and the newly-married pair go direct from the church to their own house, or perhaps into the country for a month or so to pass the honeymoon.

On moving into a neighborhood the new-comer is expected to send his card to all the residents on each side of the street in the block on which he lives, these being considered his neighbors.

It is not unusual if any one sees you pass wearing some article of dress which especially pleases them, to send a servant with their compliments bearing a tray and request you to send it for them to look at and probably to imitate. Should you express admiration for anything of theirs, it is at once placed at your disposition. Of course, this is merely a form of compliment which you are never expected to take in earnest.

Young girls are always conducted to and from school by an attendant, and no lady goes into the street unaccompanied, as it is not considered *comme il faut*, and she would, by so doing, expose herself to the possibility of being spoken to by any man who met her un-

accompanied. Neither would a man be found
visiting a lady alone (unless he were privileged
by his great seniority of years), nor would he
detain her in conversation in the parlor of a
hotel, lest by so doing he should compromise
not only her but himself as well. You cannot
walk or ride out alone with a man—there is
safety only in numbers, and a *tête-à-tête* is not
admissible except when the opportunity presents itself in the midst of company. *Les
convenances* are rigidly observed. Yet this is
a country where love is in the air, and the
winged god, ever watchful, has his shafts
always ready, and with unerring aim plants
them where he wills, despite the barriers that
hedge about his divinity only to increase and
stimulate his persistency.

Although a lady may go out into the street
with nothing over her head or shoulders, either
in a volante or walking, she would not lift up
her trailing skirts to save them from the dust,
lest by so doing she expose to view her pretty
foot or ankle; yet a Spanish officer told me that
he fell in love with the lady of his admiration
at first sight on seeing her foot as she de-
scended from a volante at El Caney. She,

with her family, came to the hotel where we were both stopping, and although he did not understand a word of French, nor she a word of Spanish, I had the pleasure of seeing the rapid *dénouement* of their mutual infatuation, and by receiving from both their confidences, thus helping in bringing about the consumation of their betrothal. In a short time she with her family sailed for France, and the young comandante had masses said at the cathedral for their safe journey across the ocean. Although I cannot complete this little romance by saying he followed her to France and married her, as I left myself soon after, yet I have no doubt that the little foot that walked into his heart so emphatically, did not relinquish its possession, but kept him fast under its tiny weight, till not only the foot itself, but the whole of its possessor became the crowning joy of the soldier's life.

Creole women in general are not intellectual, though those who are sent away to be educated have many accomplishments. They have great artistic perceptions, are quick to learn, and having natural ability for music, they are fine musicians, but early marriages and many chil-

dren soon fill up a woman's life with domestic
duties, and a natural indolence does not con-
duce to study.   They excel in all social graces
—possessing charming affability, with cordial,
affectionate manners, which render them very
fascinating.   Fond of dress and finery—the
warm climate being conducive to many changes
in the filmy fabrics, which are manufactured
especially for the Cuban market—they require
a large assortment of gowns; for no one who
has any regard for her reputation for being
well dressed would be seen at theater, ball or
opera in a dress that had been worn before.

At the theater and opera ladies never occupy
the orchestra chairs, but must always have a
box.   The chairs are reserved for the men, who
engage them for the season, just as are the
boxes.

The low, open-work gilded railings and par-
titions being all open, the whole toilette is displayed, back and sides as well as front.   A
constant movement of the beautiful fans that
with a soft click of pearl on pearl and ivory on
ivory, as their jeweled sticks are folded back
and forth with a swinging motion peculiar only
to Spanish women, is heard all over the house

like the fluttering wings of a flock of birds or the rustle of the wind among the trees.

The beauty of the Cuban woman soon passes its meridian. She either becomes immensely stout or shrinks and shrivels like a piece of parchment. Her pale complexion becomes brown and dark, and she settles down into an old woman, unredeemed by intellect or intelligence; even as the gorgeous flowers of her own country which, after they have been gathered a few hours, wither and curl up into a blackened mass, devoid of all beauty and fragrance.

VI.

A DAY IN A CUBAN HOME.

BEING invited to spend the day with some friends, escorted by the son, who had been educated in the United States, I went over, curious to see what a day passed in a Cuban *ménage* would be like.

A most cordial and gracious reception was given me, and the first thing asked was: "C——, have you not brought a blusa to put on?" The blusa is the usual indoor dress worn by Cuban ladies at home; and a very appropriate and comfortable garment it is for this extremely warm climate. It is usually made of very thin muslin or batiste, full and wide, hanging loose from a band or yoke, and floats, unconfined by belt or sash, with perhaps only a single garment beneath it. The sleeves, being loose and flowing, with the open neck, also contribute to the coolness and comfort of the dress. A little addition of lace or em-

broidery about the neck and sleeves and down
the front gives a touch of elegance to what,
under other conditions, might have an air of
slovenliness. When the blusa is made *décolleté*
a light handkerchief is thrown across the
shoulders or pinned about the neck. Thus at-
tired the Cuban matron is always considered
amply dressed to receive whatever visitors may
present themselves.

The young lady immediately brought out
one of her own pretty white muslin blusas, and
asking me if I did not wish to take off my cor-
set and make myself comfortable, helped me
to put it on.

This struck me as a most sensible arrange-
ment, for the long, warm day in prospect was
thus denuded of some of its terrors. The
mamma and the señorita were both in blusas,
and I seemed to feel myself more at home in
my borrowed blusa than in the grenadine I had
taken off. The various younger children were
playing about, untrammeled by garments of
any sort.

There were no carpets on the floors, no upholstered furniture of any sort. The door
from the street opened directly into the parlor,

while the great windows down to the floor contributed light and air in abundance.

The rocking-chairs, which are the first necessity in the furnishing of a Cuban house, were ranged in the center of the room, in two rows facing each other, between the outer door and those opening onto the patio or court, in the center of the house, and onto which all the rooms open.

Here, rocking and fanning and chatting, we sit in view of the street, in view of the court till breakfast is announced.

After an elaborate *menu* of many courses and much smoking, in which the ladies join, we find we are quite advanced beyond the middle of the day.

A visitor spending the day does not interfere with the usual afternoon siesta, for you are made so much at home that you feel no hesitation in joining in the needed rest.

Late in the afternoon, as the hour for dinner draws near, the children are clothed; the host goes out into the patio and refreshes himself, bathing face and hands with entire nonchalance in full view of us all.

The young gentleman, having already

ordered his horse, which was brought out from his stable somewhere in the rear, mounts him and rides though the parlor where we are and out into the street.

My hostess smoked as much as her husband and son, and the little five-year-old boy also seemed to enjoy his cigarette.

In no way were the usual habits of the family disturbed by the entertainment of a visitor. The simple *ménage* was all in view; there was no straining for effect, but the natural, kindly ease and courtesy made it impossible to be otherwise than delighted with the atmosphere of cordiality which reigned in this household.

Cots are usually the beds most generally preferred, though brass and iron are sometimes seen, these latter being curtained with lace or netting against the mosquitoes.

The cots during the day are folded up and set aside out of view, and at night are easily placed wherever desired; with a linen sheet thrown over them, and a pillow added, they are ready for occupancy.

After an abundant and pleasant dinner the smoking continued up to the moment of my de-

parture, my hostess saying she even took her
cigar to bed with her, smoking until she fell
asleep, and if it remained unfinished, she laid
it on a chair near the bed, so she might resume
it on awaking in the morning, and enjoyed the
picking it up again and making her morning
toilette with it still between her lips.

I came away with reiterated invitations to
come again soon, and whenever I liked, impressed with the feeling that the assurance
always given you when visiting a Cuban that
"Usted esta in su casa" (you are in your owner
house), in this case at least, was not an empty
compliment.

VII.

STREETS IN SANTIAGO.

THE streets in Santiago are narrow, dirty, badly paved, even when paved at all, and uninviting; though they are not so bad as in Havana, where in some instances, they are so narrow that in passing a carriage, when walking, one is obliged to squeeze himself close up against the houses in order to get by and to drive up one street and down another in order to ride at all. The city being built upon an incline, many of them are steep and laborious of ascent, and equally disagreeable in descent.

The sidewalks are narrow, in some instances not more than two can walk abreast—while many streets have no sidewalks at all; the wretched pavement of huge stones, painful to walk over, reaching from house to house on either side.

The walks are raised a foot or more above the road, and sometimes the step down is so abrupt that you are willing to accept the ex-

tended hand of some gallant cavalier, who, in
passing, extends his own to facilitate your descent.   Stranger though he be, an attention of
this kind offered is only considered a passing
civility, and he raises his hat, politely bowing
as he leaves.

Large square stones are left in the pavement
at intervals of from one to two feet apart, a
foot or foot and a half high, so that in the
rainy season when the waters rush down in
floods over the streets pedestrians may be en-
abled to cross by means of stepping from one
stone to another.   There are no trees on the
streets, shade being dependant upon the low,
closely built houses.

Architecturally Santiago is very disappoint-
ing; the houses, with few exceptions being
plain, flat one-story edifices without cellars,
without chimneys, without windows, often
without any elevation above the street, one step
only being necessary in making an entrance.
I should not say without windows, for the great
iron-barred openings, extending from floor
almost to ceiling, are provided with inside
shutters that can be closed in case of storm,
and in which is inserted one pane of thick,

opaque glass that admits light, but is not transparent enough to see through.

Chimneys are not needed, as there is no occasion for fires in this superheated atmosphere, and the cooking is done out of doors, upon brick ranges over small, square openings for burning charcoal.

On account of the frequency of earthquakes the houses rarely are more than one or two stories in height. Heavy timbers are planted several feet deep in the ground at the corners of the building, and at intervals of several feet apart, and these intervening spaces are filled in with stone, brick or adobe, as the case may be; often the tile roof projecting over and making a veranda or corridor, as they say in Cuba, on the front, as also over the patio around which the house is built. Thus, when an earthquake comes, the houses sway from side to side under the shock, and though there is a great creaking of timbers and a grinding, jarring sensation, like the movement of a boat going through the locks, as it is bumped up against the sides by the boiling waters; though a sickening sensation invades your inmost being as the ground heaves and rumbles be-

neath your foundations and your pictures swing
out of plumb, and the bric-a-brac tilts and tot-
ters on its base, yet, when it has passed you
find your walls still standing, your floors still
beneath your feet, and your roof still over
your head, thanks to this precautionary way
of building.

All your neighbors have run out into the
street crying: "Misericordia!" and you are
left with a nervous, apprehensive fear that
another shock is likely to follow.

These one-story houses are built compactly,
contiguous one to another, the separating par-
titions often extending up only as far as the
top of the room, leaving a space between that
and the roof, which permits the sounds from
your next neighbor's house being quite easily
heard.   There being no plastered ceilings, only
the painted rafters boarded over, and upon
which the tiles are laid, a somewhat bare, unfinished aspect is given to the interiors of
Cuban houses.   The floors are of marble, tile
or wood, without carpets or matting, on account of the numerous insects which abound.

Rows of rocking-chairs, standing opposite
each other, are placed down the middle of the

room, and, besides a piano, very few other
articles of furniture are needed.

The patio is the most attractive part of the
house, being usually surrounded by broad corridors, out on to which all the rooms open.
Vines, trees and plants make it charming; the
bright red pomegranate, with its dark, pol-
ished green leaves; yellow limes, and darker
oranges, hanging from more lofty trees; the
banana, with its broad leaves breaking into
narrow slits as it reaches up higher and higher,
with its one stem of fruit like a great red heart
bursting open with its hundred small bananas
clustering close to the stem; climbing jasmines, with starry blossoms that make the air
fragrant as soon as evening falls; parrots chat-
tering and paroquets hopping about among the
branches of the trees, a fountain playing in
the midst and children sprawling about, often
with nothing on but a pair of shoes, or possi-
bly a cambric shirt, rolled up into a wisp
about the waist and tucked into a knot behind,
so that the nurse may take hold of it; little
black children of the servants and the white
ones all playing together, there being much
more familiarity between mistress and servants
there than here—such is the ensemble.

But to come back to the front of the house:
its great doors swing open wide enough for the
volante to be driven through into the hall,
where it is kept. In one of these great doors
there is usually a smaller door for persons to
pass through, and this is the only entrance for
everything and everybody that comes into the
house, from the governor down to the mules.

All houses are painted in light, and generally,
bright colors; blues, yellows, reds, and sometimes, when they are of two stories, the lower
will be of one color and the upper another. It
is all in harmony with the gorgeous, tropical
landscape, and the eye soon becomes accustomed to the deep ochres, dull reds, pale blues
and pinks, which seem to vie with the flowers
and foliage and rank vegetation, and in a
measure atones for the want of architectural
beauty that would otherwise leave these narrow, steep, uncomfortable streets bare and un-
attractive.

The banks, the Casino, the clubs, and some
rich private residences, are built of marble,
have two stories, and some are in Oriental
style, and are of very elaborate architecture.

Several streets, like the Tivoli, for instance,

are so much higher than the one next, on account of the steep rise in the land on this side hill, that they have the appearance of terraces, from whence one looks down upon the roofs of the streets below as well as far out over the lower portions of the town and away over the bay. Nothing more fascinating can be conceived than thus, from your second story, to sit on your own corridor late in the afternoon and enjoy the sweep of view that stretches out before you.

In various parts of the city small plazas are interspersed, with shade trees, fountain, and the sweet scented jasmine, they afford breathing places where in the evening people may gather to refresh themselves.

Thus the ensemble of the city, viewed from the landing at the pier as the houses extend quite down to the water's edge and away up on to the green hills, or I might say mountains behind it, presents a most romantic and picturesque appearance with its multicolored walls and red tiled roofs gleaming out among the royal palms and feathery cocoa trees against its green background, capped with purple, and all overarched with the cloudless unchanging blue of skies that never frown.

VIII.

A VISIT TO THE HACIENDA OF SANTA ANITA.

Having been invited by Mr. O'C—— to pass
Christmas on his estate, we were obliged to
get up between three and four o'clock in the
morning to take the early train which would
carry us part way there. Thus for the first
time I saw the sun rise in this tropical country. Stopping at the market on our way to the
depot we got a cup of black coffee to fortify us
for our early journey, and were soon on board
the train for El Christo.

As we drew out into the open country all
vegetation was dripping wet as from a recent
shower. But not a cloud was in sight, and we
learned that it was only the usual heavy dew
that had drenched everything so copiously and
hung with glowing drops every leaf and branch
and stem.

The rank luxuriousness of vegetation was as-
tonishing—a perfect tangle of tropical growth.
Flowers and plants unknown greeted our eyes

on every side, with gorgeous blossoms and trailing vines, all glistening in the early sunshine, still bedewed with the abundant moisture of the previous night.

At the end of our journey by rail we found horses and mules sent by our host awaiting us. The ladies took off their hoopskirts, which were put into a bag and with other baggage packed onto the mules. Exchanging our dresses for riding habits we mounted the saddle horses, and soon all were ready for the upward and onward journey.

The Cuban horses have a peculiar gait, which I have found in no others, between a trot and a canter, which gives one no jolt, but is rather a rocking movement producing no fatigue.

Our course lay over no traveled roads, but across estates, through plantations, under orange groves and through fields of sugar cane. Our sure-footed horses scrambled along, picking their way over fallen trees and rolling logs, rough stones and wild climbing weeds, up hill and down dale, till at last we came in sight of Santa Anita. Here at the threshold of his hospitable abode our delightful host awaited us.

We had been prepared for a not very elaborate *ménage*, for Mr. O'C—— had told us when he invited us that it was hardly the place to invite señoras to, as he had never yet built his house there, though always intending to, and was only living in a rough way with his bachelor sons, his engineers, servants, etc., and had no ladies in his family.

We dismounted before a wide veranda with solid brick floor, long enough and wide enough as I afterwards discovered to serve as a dining room.   Upon the wooden railing in front were disposed the saddles of our several horses, which were then led away by various colored grooms, while we seated ourselves upon the leather covered chairs and settees to rest after our long ride.

The room assigned to me (as being the one least accustomed to roughing it) proved to be the room usually occupied by Mr. O'C——, opening out from his library, of which I remarked little except the several large handsome mahogany bookcases which lined the sides and were filled with a choice collection of works in many languages.   Upon the table were reviews and periodicals of all countries, and newspapers from New York, London, and Paris.

This residence, for I cannot call it a house, was merely a huge pavilion or circular roof of tiles resting upon wooden supports without walls and without foundation. Here and there at various points around the supports, rooms had been built by boarding up a square space beneath the roof like a box stall.

The greater part of the area under this immense tile canopy was occupied by the fires and kettles required in the process of making the sugar.

A little railway from the cane field brought the long stalks up to an engine stationed a few feet away from the veranda, where it was ground up, and in a few moments issued forth in a liquid state and ran out into a conduit or canal, where long ranges of iron kettles were waiting to receive it, and where after due process of boiling and drying it was transformed into sugar.

On opening my shutter in the morning, for window there there was none, my room was invaded by a great fog of steam arising from the boiling kettles with which the whole place was filled.

I hastily closed my blind to shut out this

steam that was wetting everything, and made my way out onto the veranda in search of fresh air.

The men of our party who had been early risers, and before going out had fortified themselves with cognac and a cup of black coffee against the early morning air, were just beginning to come in after their tramp around the estate.

Toward nine o'clock the table was set out on the veranda, and the first meal of the day called the "tent à pied" was served. There was chocolate, *café au lait*, rolls, warm bread of various kinds, pickled oysters, Westphalia sausage, stuffed olives, cold meats, everything in greatest profusion, all served by colored servants.

Although it was the 25th of December, and the temperature was the lowest I had experienced since I had been on the island, we found it quite agreeable taking our meal al fresco at this early hour.

At one o'clock came breakfast—an elaborate meal of many courses and good wines, served by many servants, and it was evident if our host did live in a house with no walls nor win-

dows, he required the services of a good cook
and supplied his larder with the delicacies of
many lands.

As the table on the veranda commanded a
view of the sugar-boiling and all the negroes
engaged in the process, it was not unusual for
our host to call out in French or Spanish to
them, in the midst of the chatter over the
glasses and cigars which made the meals under
this hospitable roof a long period of sociability
as well as conviviality.

Dinner was served at 7 o'clock, and as
course after course came on with its accompaniment of choicest wine, its rich and varied
menu and charming conversation in alternat-
ing English, Spanish, French and German,
time sped on unheeded. Nine o'clock came,
10 o'clock came and found us still at the
table, the colored servants darting in and out,
bringing in from no one knows where the
steaming viands.

Doves were perching upon the rafters above
our heads and circling tamely about, cooing
and flapping their wings in seeming satisfac-
tion at the scene.

Great dogs were stretched out in close prox-

imity with noses on their paws, apparently enjoying the savory odors.

In the ruddy glow of the red fires beneath
the seething caldrons stood out the dusky
forms of the negroes with their long-handled
dippers scooping up the boiling syrup, the
white steam rising in transparent clouds, partially obscuring them with its filmy drapery,
making a weird picture against the darkness
of the night without.

All this formed a singular accompaniment to
the elegant assemblage around the hospitable
board of the man who, living far from city or
neighbors, found within his own domain all the
elements of lavish entertainment.

The next morning we were surprised by
a cavalcade of ladies and gentlemen who appeared and dropped in to make a morning call
on their way to some distant plantation.

They needed no urging to accept an invita-
tion to remain and take breakfast; evidently
Santa Anita's reputation for hospitality was so
well known that visitors were always sure of
receiving a hearty welcome.

Around this hospitable board there was
always room enough for half a dozen or more

additional guests, and though neighbors were distant and scattered, they did not fail, when an opportunity presented itself, of making the most of such rare pleasures as came in their way.

In this land of leisure and slowness, where everything is put off till "mañana," there is time always to be sociable even in the morning, to sit at length over the table and laugh and chat, as the wreaths of smoke curl upward from fragrant cigars, with no thought of hurry or work, but with a sybaritic enjoyment of the present moment that makes life seem a long, long summer day.

On the third day we left Santa Anita, having had a taste of new and unique experiences, and brought away with us pictures in strong and glowing colors that afford unspeakable pleasure as we recall them even now from afar away down the dim vista of time.

IX.

SAINTS IN SANTIAGO.

As in all Catholic countries nearly every day in the year is a saint day, that is to say a holiday.   In the calendar they are marked as single cross days, which signifies a half holiday, or with two crosses, which means an all-day holiday.

All these holidays are instituted by the church and religiously observed by attendance at the various services, and also by a suspension of business, and much social festivity, which it is always considered proper to indulge in after the religious duties of the day have been duly performed.

Instead of celebrating the aniversary of the day of one's birth, they celebrate the day of the saint upon which it falls; for in the naming of a child some saint is always included, often several, as for instance "Frederic Maria

Joseph de la Tehada,'' or "Anita Jesus Maria de los Angeles Jiraudy.''

A child is baptized very soon after it is born, when but a few days old. Its padrinos or sponsors are chosen, and accompanied by the father it is carried to church, where in the presence of invited friends the baptism takes place. The occasion of a baptism is always attended by a gathering of youngsters outside and around the doors of the church, to whom, on coming out, the father of the newly-made Christian throws a quantity of small silver coins which are vigorously scrambled for and picked up by the gamins who have been patiently awaiting them.

Cards announcing the advent of the newly born, to which are attached a ribbon, with the name and all the saints' names and date of birth printed upon it, and at the end of which hangs a small gold coin, are sent around to intimate friends as souvenirs of congratulation upon the happy event.

As soon as the child is old enough to be taken out it is sent forth, beautifully dressed in a long robe of thinnest and finest white batiste elaborately trimmed with lace, its sleeves caught up with jeweled clasps, and a chain and little locket about the neck, lying upon a pillow in the arms of its black nurse to be viewed by admiring friends.

The day of Corpus Christi is one of the most gorgeous celebrations of all the *fête* days. This occurs early in June, and elaborate preparations are made for it long in advance. Modistes and couturiers are busy over the making up of costumes ordered expressly for that occasion; many of the señoras having also imported their dresses from Paris or Madrid for the occasion, it being indispensable to be dressed in an entirely new costume, and, indeed, in two, or perhaps three, in the course of the day.

The procession bearing the holy effigy leaves the cathedral with much pomp and display, escorted by many prominent personages in both Church and State. The streets through which it passes are decorated with flags and gorgeous hangings, in some instances forming a complete and continuous canopy which reaches from side to side across the narrow street.

In the windows and balconies of every house

are assembled parties of ladies who have been invited to see the procession pass. Here are displayed the fine toilettes, which for weeks past have been the subject of so much conversation and solicitous consultation. These invited guests usually remain to breakfast, and the gentlemen make frequent promenades up and down before the windows and balconies, enjoying the display of beauty and elegance afforded by the occasion.

Later in the afternoon another toilette is made, and the streets are filled with a procession of volantes, with their gayly appareled occupants which are driven round and round through the decorated and canopied streets and finally debouching upon the Alameda, wind up with the usual promenade to the music of the marine band, and the gaze of admiration of less fortunate onlookers.

Sunday is the day par excellence for the best functions both at the opera and theater, as also the *soirées dansantes* at the Casino.

A good Catholic, having been to his early mass, considers the rest of the day well passed in social conviviality with his friends and neighbors. A lady may occupy herself with her crocheting or embroidery, if it is taken up only as a pastime, while she would feel condemned were she obliged to do any work from necessity.

About midsummer comes St. John's, or as it is called San Juan's day. This is a day given over to all sorts of grotesque jollity, to the accompaniment of musical instruments of all sorts, the firing of torpedoes and fire-crackers; and hilarity of the most noisy description is freely indulged in; the colored portion and the lower classes contributing the greater part with their processions, frolicking and the wildest kind of dancing of all sorts. This being their especial holiday, it presents at some points a wild bacchanalian scene, such as only the hot blood and extravagant, saturnalian temperament of the dark race can portray.

The first of November is "All Saints' Day," the second is the "Dia de los Muertos," or "All Souls' Day," when the graves of the departed are visited and decorated, and masses said for the repose of their souls, and is one of the most rigidly respected. No carriages are seen in the streets; not a piano is heard, and over all an air of unusual, all-pervading quiet reigns.

In Santiago everything is named after some saint; not only streets and churches, plazas and barracks, but even clubs and *cafés*, fortresses and islands, as also are estates, rivers and cemetaries. Indeed, a name without the prefix of "saint" would be difficult to find.

Being about to take a journey across the ocean I was asked to what saint I was going to commend myself before setting out; but as I could not, with truth, say I had arranged with any for safe conduct, I know I was an object of solicitude and commiseration on the part of my more believing friends.

X.

INSECTS AND MOONLIGHT.

HERE the sun leaps from his morning couch without the lingering dalliance that in the North makes the cold, gray dawn that deepens slowly into the golden glory of its full awakening. With a bound he is above the horizon, and his flaming breath fills the earth with his torrid warmth, and all nature is aglow with his fervid magnetism.

Quickly the soft mists break and disperse from mountain-top and valley, and sea, and stream, and rivulet stand revealed in all their blue and green and foam-flecked loveliness. The bud of yesterday is now a full blown flower, clad in gorgeous colors, and shedding her perfume lavishly, as incense before her god. Myriads of insects disport themselves in the shining rays and fill the air with their tiny hum.

The red flamingo, with outstretched wings, lazily preens himself as he stalks daintily along with his fine slender needle-like legs, down to the water's edge, where, after his early sip, he stands, with one foot drawn up under his wing gazing down upon his own reflection in the water below.

Slender green and gold lizards climb up the tree trunks and the brown chameleons changing color with every new shadow, disport themselves harmlessly on the projecting walls and balconies.

"As you rock back and forth in your rocking-chair a crunching sound arrests your attention, and you find you have unwittingly rocked upon a scorpion, whose lobster-like claws and long tail may measure six inches, and sometimes among the laces in your bureau drawers you may espy one of their black tails, raised in warning; and it is well enough to shake your shoes before putting them on in the morning to make sure that you do not come in contact with one in your first steps toward your morning toilette.

Whole cordons of tiny red ants, with sentinel at either end, are likely to line the walls of your room from ceiling to floor and across to the plate containing any fruit or eatables or drinkables left unawares upon your table—a constant line of comers and goers, making an unbroken chain of small unconquerable enemies, always at hand to prey upon your delicacies.

Multitudes of fleas introduce themselves unceremoneously between the interstices of your open work stockings, and if you are sensible to their punctures make life a burden until you become accustomed to them.

Cockroaches of magnificent proportions, of glossy brownness, huddle behind your bureaus and buffets, and must be swept out now and then, by regiments.

Tarantulas and centipedes are sometimes encountered, and to the student of entomology there are always new species to be discovered.

Butterflies as large as bats, of gorgeous, spotted green, as also the somber, black-winged ones, whose presence portends death, and fills a mother's heart with terror if one rests upon the pillow of her child, are seen.

When the sun has lowered his heavy velvet curtains before his face, and in the dark blue dome the stars come thickly forth, the innumerable fireflies flutter out from every blade and spear, and the great cocuyo, queen of fireflies, appears, emitting electric flashes of greenish light from breast and eyes and back, till the whole of its dark shell is hidden out of sight as an ugly face is sometimes illuminated and transfigured by a flash of genius.

One can see what o'clock it is by the watch, or, with two or three under a glass, may see to read, and sometimes they are sewed under tarletan or muslin dresses to add a touch of brilliancy to an evening toilette.

As you float at evening in your faluja out over the waters of the tranquil bay propelled by the steady strokes of stalwart rowers, as the rythmic oars rise and fall they cleave into a flaming deep, alive with tiny phosphorescent insects which gild the oars and fall in golden splashes back into the waves again.

Leaning back against the cushioned rail you see the great Southern Cross clear and distinct in the heavens. The great silver moon seems twice its size at full, and so near that you almost shrink from its closeness, and feel inclined to raise your fan between it and your face, and as you glide about between the great ships anchored there, looking below the water line, can distinctly see the colored stripes thereon painted, so great is the illuminating power of the moonlight upon and below the water. Yet within all the witchery and fascination of this wonderful moonlight there lurks a counter-charm of dangerous power.

It is not considered prudent to sit long where it falls serenely upon you, lest you find a headache settling down over you; and young children if taken out at night are carefully guarded from its rays by having an umbrella carried over them.

Sitting out upon your balcony, you choose a corner which affords a spot of shade rather than subject yourself to the malign influence that counter-balances the pleasure of its full enjoyment.

Fish or meat after a few hours' exposure to to its rays become unfit for use.

To sleep in the moonlight is fraught with unhappy consequences—contortion of the features, if not a disturbed condition of the brain ensuing; as upon the unconscious sleeper, enwrapped in its silvery sheen, silently and mysteriously under the cover of night its poisoned arrows unerringly swoop down leaving their fatal impress upon their innocent victim.

XI.

THE SPANISH LION AND THE BLUE FAN.

LATE in the afternoon there was an unusual stir and commotion below in the hotel. Arola asked Geneveva, her faithful colored friend and servant, what it was all about.

"Oh, mademoiselle! Buque just come in—great heap mens—from Santo Domingo—en pile officiers——"

Looking down from the corridor on to the patio below Arola saw numbers of uniformed officers with swords dangling from their belts and spurs clanking at their heels as they strode hither and yon across the tiled floor and up and down the stone stairs, while soldiers and assistants were bringing in equipages, portmanteaus and impedimenta of various description, and piling it up against columns in doorways, and in all sorts of inconvenient places, until our usually attractive patio began to look like a military barrack, with all this additional influx of Spanish soldiery.

Madame Adela, in flying blusa, flapping slippers and gay bandana, was bustling about as fast as her great avoirdupois would allow, unlocking doors, apportioning rooms, and dispatching Juan, Eduardo, Melina and Cæsar in various directions to prepare the rooms, carry up the trunks and provide for the comfort of her newly-arrived guests, while Don Eugenio, her white husband, but in no sense master of the house, meekly carried out her instructions in all matters, stooping in the meantime every now and then to catch up in his arms the little naked three-year-old negreto Eduardo (who, like a little black puppy dog, was running around under everybody's feet, in everybody's way), and giving him a hearty squeeze and kiss, much to the amusement as well as disgust of some of the on-lookers.

Madame Adela owned her husband, as well as the hotel, and, being the landed as well as monetary proprietor, did not scruple on some occasions (when Don Eugenio forgot to come in at proper hours or indulged too much in his favorite beverages) to turn the key in the door of his room, and keep him in solitary confinement a day or two, until he came back to a sense of his marital responsibilities.

Although Don Eugenio was white and Madame Adela mulatto, she came of good French descent on her father's side, which showed itself in her gentle manners and kindly, dignified bearing, that won the universal respect and appreciation of all who were domiciled beneath her roof.

This was an invasion, indeed! The *salon*, patio, corridors, halls, and stairways, all overflowing with these returned militaires, fresh from an encounter with insurgents in Santo Domingo, from whence the "Regiment de Espagna" had just disembarked.

Arola looked down with dismay upon this taking possession of our usually orderly, quiet hotel, to whose homelike tranquil atmosphere she was so accustomed that any disturbing influence was most unwelcome. It was as though a rough wind had swept across the placid waters of the bay, stirring up into rough waves its peaceful depths, setting all the barks tossing and rocking restlessly upon its surface.

As Arola took her seat at dinner she saw up and down the length of the table opposite as also at her side the various types of the Spanish race, with all their arrogant consciousness of superiority, their pride of birth and pride of conquest, tempered with easy grace and debonair, chivalric manners, and warm magnetic temperament, which at once swept us all within the radius of its influence, subtly permeating with its atmosphere the susceptible recipients of its fascination.

The atmosphere at once became electric, currents darted here and there, creating sympathy or producing opposition as they flashed in upon the new elements just encountered.

Tall, serious and dignified as a young palm, the sedate and valiant Colonel Sandoval chanced to occupy the seat at the right of the head of the table, next to the sympathetic Consul, who, although he had never got further in the Spanish language than "Buenos dias, como esta usted!" and "Muchas gracias," nevertheless, by his cheerful, gracious ways, had won the title of "Muy Sympatico" from all who knew him, and was always the favorite neighbor at table or wherever good company was desired.

Discussion ran high, and anecdotes were recounted of the late experiences in the recent Santo Domingo outbreak of one officer in particular, whose extravagant exploits and reckless daring was the theme of comment in every action; evidently he had cut a wide swath wherever he went, and consequences of deep import were left behind.

On arriving at a new place in a few days he was master of the dialect; in battle was always in the thickest of the fight, at the bivouac he was always the foremost drinker; could tell the best story and sing the best song, and with holy horror the dignified Sandoval exclaimed: "When I went to my room I found his assistant setting up his bed there!"

"Well! Did you not order him out?"

"Oh, no! I knew the best thing for me to do was to keep quiet. He had been out to supper with some friends, and, coming back late, found the door fastened, and with a banging and clatter enough to break it down he nearly scared Juan out of his senses, when he finally succeeded in rousing him sufficiently to open it."

Thus, his advent into our hotel was followed by the characteristic whirlwind he usually brought in his wake.

Arola's curiosity was much stimulated by all

these revelations with wonder as to what sort
of a personality this stormy petrel could possess.   Her imagination busied itself with pic-
turing this altogether new type, that seemed
instantly to have created a peculiar attraction
for this strange unknown in the quiet American girl, who had listened to all the varied
comments upon this rough and arrogant Aragonese.

Coming into breakfast Sunday morning diagonally across from her seat at table and near
the dignified Sandoval, Arola beheld a new
face, with a wide, high forehead, from which
the closely cut, dark hair was brushed severely
back, deep, blue-gray eyes, looking frankly
out from beneath heavy, dark brows; a fine
Roman nose with expanding nostrils, betoken-
ing a fiery, haughty temperament, surmounted
a heavy, dark mustache and closely-trimmed
beard, that outlined a chin indicating firmness
of purpose and unyielding will.   A grave,
almost sad, expression pervaded this face in repose; strength and almost severity were the
characteristics indicated in its lines.

Suddenly Arola became aware of an intense
gaze being fixed upon her, and looking up in

the direction from which she felt it, beheld the eyes of the Aragonese fixed seriously upon her.

His remarks were addressed to his companions in arms on either hand, but his eyes were speaking a language of their own while they held the attention of Arola, who in vain tried to withdraw her own.

Presently a mingling of phrases as well as regards began to fall upon her outward ear that indicated they were intended for her, as, in answer to some one, he remarked:

"Yes! I am a very capricious person, and I will go all lengths to arrive at the consummation of my caprices. I am *never* defeated."

Thus saying he threw himself back a little, partially behind the one next him, from whence, unobserved, he could watch the effect of his words upon her.

As was her custom, while her father and the gentlemen remained chatting over their cigars, she arose and retired from the table; passing into the *salon*, she seated herself by a window opening on to the corridor, which commanded a view of the bay and the signal station. Even from this distance she was still conscious that those eyes were upon her, as the Aragonese continued his conversation and smoking at the table.   Presently a footstep coming toward her attracted her attention, and a whiff of fragrant smoke was wafted toward her, as the stalwart figure of the Aragonese strode across the *salon*, and, passing through the open door out on to the corridor, took up a position opposite the window near which she was seated, and leaning against one of the columns, in a loud whisper, said:

"You are very cruel, very ungrateful."

Arola turned a startled, surprised look upon him, astonished at his thus addressing her, and he repeated his remark.

"But señor," she said, "you do not know me—we are strangers."

"Ah!   But I do know you.   I have been here more than twenty-four hours, and I have observed you closely.   Did you not see I was always looking at you at the table?"

"But I supposed that might be accidental."

"There are no accidents with me.   In you I have found the one being I adore—that I have sought for in vain.   I am alone in the world; I have led a wild life.   Of all the women I have met, none have I loved till now."

The *salon* began to fill up as the others left the table. The conversation was broken off. Some one asked Arola to play, and she went to the piano and commenced playing in a half dreamy way some Spanish boleros and dances. Presently she became aware that some one was leaning over the instrument, closely watching her, and a low voice at her side was pouring out, in unbroken monologue, the history of his life, thus taking advantage of the accompanying music which drowned the low tones of his voice, making a secluded oasis among the general conversation.

Arola scarcely saw him. Her eyes followed her hands upon the keys, while his fervent words fell upon her ears and burned through into her mind. It was like a torrent of flame that swept over her in all its impetuosity. A strange lassitude began to creep over her; the slender fingers began to resist her will, and she arose from the piano, and, escaping from this new influence that was fast gaining ascendency over her, endeavored to throw it off by shutting herself away in the retirement of her own apartment.

After dinner Arola went out onto the balcony

to enjoy the refreshing night air and the soft
moonlight. Immediately the arrogant one
was at her side, and, scanning her carefully
from head to foot, remarked:

"What means all this blue?" noticing the
soft folds of her white dress and broad blue
scarf that encircled her waist, falling to the
bottom of her skirt, and the bows of same
shade that looped up the sleeves, and even the
circlets of blue sapphires around her throat
and wrists, and the blue fan which, with
almost Spanish grace, she had learned to sway
languidly back and forth.

"What does all this signify?" taking the fan
from her hand and looking seriously down
upon her, after a few vigorous movements
handing it back to her with the partly open,
sidewise presentation which signifies "love."
"You cannot be jealous; yet blue is jeal-
ousy."

"Oh! I did not know that."

"You could not be jealous of me, for I have
but one thought. I desire but you. I find all
my happiness here between these four walls.
To me you are like the Virgin upon the high
altar, to be worshiped, idolized. You fill

me with illusions. To be thus near you, so near I might almost touch you, fills me with happiness, with emotions impossible for any other woman to inspire. For me there is naught else in the world."

"I will see the general and get permission to leave the Regiment de Espagna, which will soon leave here, and get a commission in the regiment that is stationed here. He will say: 'I know why you wish to stay here; it is on account of the little American girl.' "

"Why will he think that?"

"Because Sandoval has told him so. Sandoval knows I love you."

He took from her hand the small blue fan, and pressing it to his lips, hid it away against his breast, giving her in exchange his own that he had brought from Santo Domingo.

Quiet, sagacious, alert Sandoval of the eagle eye, was closely watching the rapidly developing chapters in this incipient romance.

Arola was conscious of his intense watchfulness that took expression in varying revelations of his passing thoughts, as he shot forth a glance of disapproval or surprise or regret at what he evidently could not alter or prevent.

From those dark, speaking eyes he would hurl forth a whole volume of emotion that needed no spoken words to convey his meaning, and Arola was conscious that she was being read like an open book by one who, with prophetic eye, looked farther and saw more than she could even imagine.

There was a peculiar tenderness and solicitude evinced in his watchfulness that drew her toward him with a feeling of undoubting confidence, and when in speaking of the "Aragonese" he called him "The Lion," it amused her and at the same time pleased her, so that she fell into the habit also of speaking of him as "The Lion;" for it seemed a fitting name for that dominating, strong, almost savage nature, that at the same time showed such moments of gentleness and humility in his approaches toward her, so much so that he seemed possessed of two natures, so subdued and almost reverent was he under the influence of her gentle nature.

Sandoval was always hovering near when "The Lion" was away; but the moment he appeared in view with a smile and a gesture which seemed to say: "Discretion is the better part of valor," he would , serenely yield his place and flee for safety.

The two men were of the same regiment, and Sandoval the superior officer, but of a refined nature, and courtly bearing characteristic of one whose family were all in the diplomatic ranks, one brother being minister to Austria, another to Mexico, but who, owing to unhappy domestic relations of his own, preferred to absent himself altogether from Spain, and for years had led a life devoid of family ties rather than live in disharmony at home.

Though in their military career Sandoval and "The Lion" were thrown into somewhat intimate relations, yet the difference in their natures was such that an invisible wall separated them, hedging them about with an impenetrable armor.

Arola was under the magnetism of two opposite natures, each of which swayed her and influenced her in different ways.

Although some of the on-lookers at this drama began to prophesy, half jokingly, half seriously, outbreaks and difficulties or disagreements among militaires, the *dramatis personœ* kept on, all unconscious of the interest and curiosity they were awakening.

One evening several officers from an Ameri-

can man-of-war presented themselves, and
Arola and her father were about going to the
Plaza with them, when "The Lion," just com-
ing in, was confronted with a new incident.

A stifled roar of displeasure, half smothered
under his mustache, for a moment disconcerted
her, betraying his evident belief in his owner-
ship of her, and unwillingness to allow others
any participation in her society. She gently
explained the situation and the necessity of
her action, and to all appearances appeased
his ruffled equanimity.

Returning at a late hour, there seemed an
unusual stir and assemblage of people around
the apartment of "The Lion;" and on inquiry,
she learned that soon after she went out, he
was seized with a severe heart attack, and had
to be carried to his room, medical help sum-
moned, and after remedies had been applied,
he was restored to consciousness, and was
being closely watched by his attendants—in
short that he was still critically ill.

Some days after she learned that the excite-
ment occasioned by her going out with her
American friends, with the effort at self-control
and suppression of his violent emotions, had

brought on this severe attack that had nearly cost him his life.

Sandoval, ever watchful, was kept in constant anxiety, and was continually saying: "Ah! Arola, you make me very unhappy. I am filled with solicitude about you. 'The Lion' will roar one day!"

But Arola seemed only to see his beautiful tawny mane and majestic proportions, and to enjoy the dominion she possessed over his savage nature with feminine perversity.

One day he remarked that she no longer carried the little Santo Domingo fan he had exchanged for her own, and on inquiring why she was not using it she frankly said that Sandoval took it up one day to fan himself and had unwittingly kept possession of it, and probably had carried it with him to his room.

At once the fire flashed from his eyes, and an expression of fierce displeasure broke upon his face. She tried to soothe him by saying: "Sandoval did not mean anything; it was purely accidental, his taking it;" but he would not be pacified.

"Sandoval is as capable of folly, as mad as any of us."

A great fear seized upon her. "Would he dare to harm him?" The thought almost paralyzed her; but the arrow had sped, the harm was done, the unforeseen had happened.

Arola lost no time in skillfully persuading Sandoval to give her back the unfortunate fan, carefully concealing from him the reason of her great anxiety to regain possession of it once more. His oft repeated "Ah! Arola, you make me very uneasy about you," seemed to have little or no effect upon her. She did not understand his solicitude.

Sometimes, passing along the corridor, she heard a footstep behind her and felt the breath of "The Lion" close to her ear, with ill suppressed ardor saying: "Now, I could give you twenty-five thousand kisses with that little bolero on. Que divina!"

Sandoval, whose all-observing eye nothing escaped, would say: "To-day the wind is from the north," or, "Now we have a south wind."

"Arola is expressive even in the clothes she wears. If I could see the dress she has laid out to put on I could tell what humor she is in before she comes to dinner."

"The Lion," after having been to the bull-fight, would bring her the banderillos he had secured from the picadores as trophies. Even in the savage enjoyment of this cruel sport, her image was always before him.

After a "Fourth of July" dinner, when the champagne flowed freely in remembrance of her native land, he improvised for her entertainment with some of his Spanish friends, in a moment of exhilaration and expansion, the "Jota Aragonese," one of the dances of his native province, to the accompaniment of its taking melody; going through its many changes and taking a leap, skip and a bound that carried him up onto and completely over the table to her great amusement and delight.

Bursts of merriment followed, and thus, another link was forged in the chain that bound her to the strange character that had so suddenly swooped down into her life; each new development proving an additional attraction.

One day an imperative order arrived from the captain-general for the regiment to embark immediately for Havana. There was no use in resistance, no time for dallying. A soldier is a machine, and has only to obey his superior. Quickly the news spread: all was hurry and bustle; preparations for departure were imperative; the steamer was to leave in a few hours.

Arola had not seen "The Lion" since he went away early in the morning to attend to his regimental duties, so she was in ignorance of this new order. She was greatly amazed when he came running upstairs in the early afternoon, and, in his impetuous way, took her in his arms exclaiming: "Arola! We are ordered to Havana! I am on the point of embarking. The troops are all on board. I have only a minute to say adieu to you and your father. This separation is inevitable, but it will be short, for as soon as I can see the captain-general at Havana I shall ask for a furlough, and in fifteen days you will see me in New York, or you will hear of my death, for I am going to challenge Sandoval; one of us must die."

Arola tried to dissuade him. She was horrified, but in vain. She was a mere straw tossed on the torrent. He did not heed nor hear her.

"You will present me to your mamma as

your future husband, and we shall never more
be separated, for you will return with me here,
Arola! You will be faithful to me? I trust
you,'' and placing a magnificent opal upon her
finger: ''You will be mine forever, forever!''
One embrace and he was gone.

Arola, like one in a dream, bewildered by
this sudden and unexpected event, stepped out
onto the corridor to look at the departing
steamer. At the same moment Don Manuel,
an old officer who had long been their next
neighbor, was leaning over the railing, observ-
ing the final movements which could be plainly
seen from where they were.

''Ah!'' he exclaimed, ''he has missed the
boat. The steamer is already under way, and
he is not halfway to the wharf. Ah! he has
dallied too long! He will be punished; he
will be imprisoned in Las Cabañas for disobey-
ing orders.''

Arola almost hoped that he had missed the
steamer, but his faithful Abrilito had secured
a small boat with efficient rowers and was im-
patiently awaiting him at the wharf, so Don
Manuel's prophecy was not verified.

Arola watched the little boat as it sped over

the water and drew up alongside the great steamer that was slowly lumbering down the bay with its freight of precious humanity.

The hotel of Madame Adela was filled with loneliness. The deserted patio and corridors no longer echoed to the tread of clanking spurs or the careless merriment of lounging officers, laughing over their campaign stories.

Arola, in this changed state of affairs, did not find the old once-prized homelike atmosphere that had reigned hitherto. It was as though a fierce wind had swept across the place and left it bare and desolate.

A few days later Arola herself was *en route* toward the cool, gray and cloudy skies of her native land. After a few months' sojourn among the undemonstrative matter-of-fact people, which seemed to her less desirable than formerly, she again returned to Santiago.

On the evening of her arrival friends flocked in to welcome her back. In recounting the things that had happened during her absence, one young man remarked:

"Oh! Arola, did you know the Aragonese was ordered to the Philippines? You know he challenged Sandoval, his superior officer, and to punish him, instead of taking away his command, his sentence was commuted to being ordered there, but on the voyage he had one of his heart attacks, and died before they reached there."

Out in midocean, out of sight of land and far from home, just as the sun was sinking below the western horizon, his loving comrades were drawn up to assist at the solemn burial service.

A sharp volley of musketry, a white cloud of smoke announced that all was over. The great ship moved on. A great heart was still. Night, with its thousand stars, hung like a pall over the tranquil deep.

Even long years after, whenever Arola gazed upon the changing colors of that glowing opal, she seemed to see reflected there the closing scene in the last act of that strange drama.

THE END.

LATE PUBLICATIONS

OF

F. TENNYSON NEELY.

LATE PUBLICATIONS

OF

F. TENNYSON NEELY.

NEELY'S
PRISMATIC LIBRARY.

Cloth, Fifty Cents.

Wife or Maid.   By M. Douglass Flattery.
Two Washington Belles.   By Lester M. del Garcia.
Forest Lily.   By James Donald Dunlop, M.D.
Omega.   By "A Reporter."
*Woman Proposes.   By Charles E. Leibold.
Richard Judkins' Wooing.   By T. Jenkins Hains.
A Runaway Couple.   By Oliver Lowrey.
*A Duel of Wits.   By E. Thomas Kaven.
In the Saddle With Gomez.   By Capt. M. Carillo.
Teeth of the Dragon.   By David Lowry.
A Cavalry Girl.   By Elizabeth Harman.
A Platonic Experiment.   (The Brown-Laurel Marriage.)
    By Landis Ayr.
Little Ethel.   By Philip H. Smith.
Though Your Sins Be as Scarlet.   By Marie Giles.
The Senator's Wife.   By Melville Philips.
An Innocent Cheat.   By T. C. DeLeon.
Even as You and I.   By Bolton Hall.
*The Modern Prometheus.   By E. Phillips Oppenheim.
Just a Summer Affair.   By Mary Adelaide Keeler.
Under the Lion's Claws.   By John N. Clarke.
A Bachelor's Box.   By T. C. DeLeon.

         * Indicates that book is illustrated.

For sale everywhere, or sent post-paid on receipt of price.

F. TENNYSON NEELY, Publisher,

96 Queen St., London.   114 Fifth Ave., N. Y.

NEELY'S
Universal Library.

NEELY'S TOURIST LIBRARY.

Paper, Twenty-five Cents.

For sale everywhere, or sent post-paid on receipt of price.

F. TENNYSON NEELY, Publisher,

96 Queen St., London.   114 Fifth Ave., N. Y.

NEELY'S
ANGLO-AMERICAN LIBRARY

Uniform Cloth Binding, 12mo., Fifty Cents Each.

Sweet Danger. By Ella Wheeler Wilcox. Illustrated.

The Captain's Romance. By Opie Read.

Remarks. By Bill Nye. Illustrated.

Dr. Carlin's Receipt Book.

The Bachelor and the Chafing Dish. By Deshler Welsh. Illustrated.

So Runs the World. By the author of "Quo Vadis."

The Treasure of the Ice. By Eugene Shade Bisbee.

Don Swashbuckler. By Eugene P. Lyle, Jr.

A Conflict of Sex. By Anna Huntington Birdsall.

The Little Blind God A-Wheel. By Sidney Howard.

Floating Fancies. Among the Weird and the Occult. By Clara H. Holmes.

The Heart of Sindhra. By Frederick Houck Law.

The City Without a Name. By Dr. H. A. Moody.

www.ingramcontent.com/pod-product-compliance
Lightning Source LLC
Chambersburg PA
CBHW020759020726
47495CB00008B/2505